HOUSES ARE MADE
OF CANDY

CANDIES GROW
IN TREES

CATICORNITOPIA

Your Guide to
ALL THINGS CATICORN

KARISSA WINTERS

ISBN 978-1-64028-311-4 (Paperback)
ISBN 978-1-64028-313-8 (Hard Cover)
ISBN 978-1-64028-312-1 (Digital)

Christian Faith Publishing, Inc.
296 Chestnut Street
Meadville, PA 16335
www.christianfaithpublishing.com

Printed in the United States of America

Your Guide to
ALL THINGS CATICORN

UNICORN HORN

HORNS CAN CHANGE COLOR

PURPLE HORN INDICATES HUNGER

HORNS CAN GLOW

You may be asking yourself what is a caticorn?

A caticorn is a cat with a magical horn, much like that of a unicorn, except its horn changes colors depending on how it's feeling. It also glows in the dark to help it see its way around at night.

The magical caticorn has pretty wings that it uses to fly. The caticorn's wings are rainbow-colored and have the most sparkly glitter ever all over them. A caticorn's wings are shaped like the wings on a butterfly. They also glow in the dark.

USING MAGICAL POWER
GLOWS IN THE DARK
WINGS LIKE A BUTTERFLY

HUGRY

NOT ENOUGH
RAINBOW TREATS

HAPPY

MUST HAVE
EATEN PLENTY OF
RAINBOW TREATS

A caticorn's fur is very, very super fluffy and rainbow-colored. A caticorn gets its rainbow coloring from all the rainbow-colored candy it eats. If it doesn't eat enough rainbow-colored candy, its fur turns white.

The caticorn lives in a very magical land located right above the clouds. It is called Caticornitopia. Caticornitopia is filled with so many wonderful things. Trees that grow candy, bushes that grow macarons, tasty rainbow-colored cotton candy clouds, and rivers made of milk. Caticornitopia also has lots of rainbows, and the caticorns even live in houses made of rainbow candy.

EXCITED

FAVORITE FOOD

HAPPY

FAVORITE FOOD

Their favorite food is the colorful macarons from the macaron bushes. It mainly likes to eat sweets and candy, especially rainbow-colored candy.

Some of the caticorns' favorite things to do are play games like hide-and-seek and take cat naps in the oh-so-fluffy and tasty cotton candy clouds. Caticorns also enjoy eating rainbow-colored candy while sliding down rainbows and floating down the milk river on donuts while sipping milk through a straw as they go.

READY TO PLAY →

EXCITED

LOVES TO EAT SUPER TASTY COTTON CANDY

UPSET

USING ITS MAGICAL POWERS!

What you really need to know is that a Caticorn is the protector of all mythical creatures, as well as rainbows (which is a super-duper important job). The caticorn has magical powers that it can use to protect the mythical creatures and rainbows. When it uses magical powers, its horn turns rainbow-colored. If it wasn't for caticorns, we wouldn't get to enjoy the gloriously magnificent rainbows as well as all of the mythical creatures.

A caticorn horn is very unique, unique indeed. It changes colors depending on how the caticorn feels. Sometimes it even turns rainbow-colored!

Here is a guide to what the colors of the caticorn horn mean. (It is very important to know how a caticorn is feeling.)

pink and glittery = happy
red = upset
yellow = excited
blue = sad
green = sick
purple = hungry
white = ready to play
rainbow = magic powers

EXCITED

SAD

HUNGRY

HAPPY

READY TO PLAY

UPSET

SICK

MAGIC POWER

Now when you look up at the sky you know to look for caticorns. Who knows, you may get lucky and see one flying around! Now that you've learned all about caticorns, you can tell everyone else about their exciting meowgical world!

About the Author

Hi! My name is Karissa Winters, but more importantly, I would like to tell you my daughter's name: Presley Winters. It is because of Presley that this book was possible. She is six and is autistic. As her mother, this gives me insight to such a beautiful and creative mind and also a glimpse into her world where a major love for all things cats exist. This is what led me to create and write about the caticorn and the magical world of the caticorns.

Our family includes my amazingly supportive husband Bryce, my lovingly sweet daughter Presley, and my special sweet boy Bowen, as well as our sweet and funny English bulldog Charlotte, our little French bulldog Claire (which my kids lovingly call her a cat dog), our very friendly cat Macaroni that likes to give kisses, and our fish Mr. Catfish. (Yes, even our fish is a CATfish.) I am so excited to have brought this story to life and most of all to be able to share it with you and your loved ones. I truly believe we were blessed with a daughter with such a passion and love for all things cats, which led me to be able to share the glorious world of caticorns with you!

CPSIA information can be obtained
at www.ICGtesting.com
Printed in the USA
LVHW072012131118
596838LV00017B/406/P